JANET S. WONG

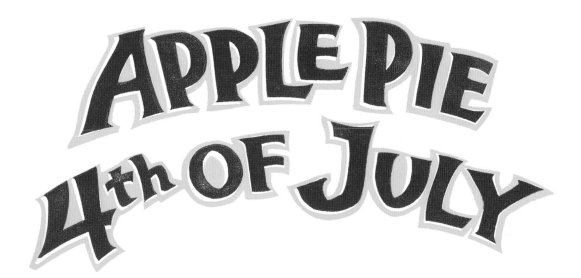

APPLE PIE 4th OF JULY

PICTURES BY
Margaret Chodos-Irvine

HARCOURT, INC.
San Diego   New York   London
Printed in Singapore

Seven days a week,
fifty-two weeks,
three hundred sixty-four days a year
(and three hundred sixty-five in a leap year),
our store is open.

Christmas is the only day we close.

Even on Thanksgiving we open the store.
Even on New Year's Day.
Even today, the Fourth of July.

I hear the parade coming this way—
boom, boom, boom.

I smell apple pie
in Laura's oven upstairs
and—

chow mein in our kitchen.
Chow mein!
Chinese food on the Fourth of July?

No one wants Chinese food
on the Fourth of July, I say.

Fireworks are Chinese, Father says,
and hands me a pan full of sweet-and-sour pork.

I hear the parade—

BOOM, BOOM, BOOM.

I hear the parade passing by.

Noon, and customers come
for soda and potato chips.

One o'clock,
and they buy ice cream.

Two o'clock.
The egg rolls are getting hard.

Four o'clock,
and the noodles feel like shoelaces.

Three o'clock.
Ice and matches.

No one wants Chinese food on the Fourth of July, I say.
Mother piles noodles on my plate.

My parents do not understand all American things.
They were not born here.

Even though my father has lived here
since he was twelve,
even though my mother loves apple pie,
I cannot expect them to know
                              Americans

do not eat Chinese food
on the Fourth of July.

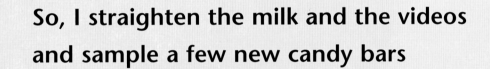

So, I straighten the milk and the videos
and sample a few new candy bars

until five o'clock,

when two hungry customers walk inside
for some Chinese food to go.

I tell them no one—no one—came,
so we ate it up ourselves

but they smell food in the kitchen
now—

and Mother walks through the swinging door
holding a tray of chicken chow mein,

and Father follows her step for step
with a brand-new pan of sweet-and-sour pork—

and three more people get in line,
eleven more at six o'clock,
nine at seven,
twelve by eight,

more and more and more and more

until it's time to close the store—

time to climb to our rooftop chairs,
way up high, beyond the crowd,

where we sit and watch the fireworks show—

and eat
our apple pie.

Requests for permission to make copies of any part of the work should be mailed to the following address:
Permissions Department, Harcourt, Inc., 6277 Sea Harbor Drive, Orlando, Florida 32887-6777.

www.harcourt.com

Library of Congress Cataloging-in-Publication Data
Wong, Janet S.
Apple pie Fourth of July/by Janet S. Wong; illustrated by Margaret Chodos-Irvine.
p. cm.
Summary: A Chinese American child fears that the food her parents are preparing to sell on the Fourth of July will not be eaten.[1. Fourth of July—Fiction. 2. Cookery, Chinese—Fiction. 3. Chinese Americans—Fiction.]
I. Chodos-Irvine, Margaret, ill. II. Title. PZ7.W842115Ap 2002
[E]—dc21   2001001313   ISBN 0-15-202543-X

A B C D E F G H   First edition

The illustrations in this book were created using a variety of
printmaking techniques on Lana printmaking paper.
The display lettering was created by Margaret Chodos-Irvine and Judythe Sieck.
The text type was set in Stone Sans Bold.
Color separations by Bright Arts Ltd., Hong Kong
Printed and bound by Tien Wah Press, Singapore
This book was printed on totally chlorine-free Nymolla Matte Art paper.
Production supervision by Sandra Grebenar and Pascha Gerlinger
Designed by Margaret Chodos-Irvine and Judythe Sieck

To Jeannette Larson, whose warmth and humor
made this story come alive
—J. S. W.

To Marty and Rosalyn Chodos, for nurturing
my creative inclinations
—M. C.-I.

How Can I Deal With...

?

Bullying

Sally Hewitt

A⁺

Smart Apple Media

Smart Apple Media is published by
Black Rabbit Books
P.O. Box 3263, Mankato, Minnesota 56002

U.S. publication copyright © 2009 Black
Rabbit Books. International copyright
reserved in all countries. No part of this
book may be reproduced in any form
without written permission from the
publisher.

Printed in the United States

Published by arrangement with the Watts
Publishing Group Ltd, London.

Library of Congress Cataloging-in-
Publication Data

Library of Congress Cataloging-in-
Publication Data

Hewitt, Sally, 1949–
    Bullying / Sally Hewitt.
    p. cm.—(Smart Apple Media. How can
I deal with...)
    Includes bibliographical references and
index.
    ISBN 978-1-59920-227-3
    1. Bullying—Juvenile literature. I.
Title.
BF637.B85H49 2009
302.3—dc22
                                    2007033962

Picture credits: John Birdsall/John
Birdsall Photography: front cover main,
7, 18. Sean Cayton/Image
Works/Topfoto: 14. Bob
Daemmrich/Imageworks/Topfoto: 26.
fotovisage/Alamy : 13. Tony
Freeman/Art Directors: 9. Spencer
Grant/Art Directors: 21. Jeff
Greenberg/Art Directors: 4. Jeff
Greenberg/ImageWorks/Topfoto: 28
Henry King/Photonia/Getty Images: 8.
R J Livermore/Art Directors: 25.
Brian Mitchell/Photofusion: 5, 19.
David Montford/Photofusion: 6.
Helene Rogers/Art Directors: 12, 24
Ellen Senisi/Image Works/Topfoto : 10,
11. 22. Bob Turner/Art Directors: 15.
Libby Welch/Photofusion: 27.

Series editor: Sarah Peutrill
Art director: Jonathan Hair
Design: Susi Martin
Picture researcher: Diana Morris
Series advisor: Sharon Lunney

**Please note: Some of the photos
in this book are posed by models.
All characters, situations, and
stories are fictitious. Any
resemblance to real persons,
living or dead, is purely
coincidental.**

9 8 7 6 5 4 3 2 1

Contents

I Feel Left Out

Maria's friends don't ask her to join in with them anymore. They say unkind things to her. When this happens, she feels lonely and left out.

Maria's Story

I used to play with my friends at recess every day. We had lots of fun.

But now, when I ask if I can play too, they say, "You can't play with us!"

In class, my friends giggle together, but they won't tell me what they are laughing about. None of them asks me over to their house after school like they used to. I feel lonely at school and at home.

Annabel didn't invite me out for her birthday. All my friends went to the movies together and had a sleepover at Annabel's house without me. I cried all that evening. I felt really left out. I don't know what I've done wrong!

What Can Maria Do?

Maria hasn't done anything wrong. Her friends aren't behaving like good friends. She can:

✔ talk about it with her teacher, her mom or dad, or her big sister, and

✔ think about how good friends behave:

- Good friends are kind to each other.
- They share with each other.
- They make each other feel happy.
- They have fun together.

What Maria Did

I told my big sister Nina. She asked two girls in my class, Lee and Kerry, if I could play with them. They are really kind and good fun. I don't mind if my old friends leave me out now. I'm much happier with my new friends.

Nina's Story

My little sister Maria wasn't happy. She didn't want to go to school. I asked her what was wrong. She told me her friends weren't being kind to her. I said they weren't being good friends.

I asked her which children in her class were kind.

She said Lee and Kerry were nice. So I helped her make friends with Lee and Kerry. I'm glad she talked to me so I could help her. She doesn't mind going to school now.

What Is Bullying?

Bullying is when someone:

- makes you unhappy and thinks it's funny,
- hurts you on purpose,
- calls you names,
- takes away your friends,
- teases you and won't stop when you ask them to, or
- steals or ruins your things.

Bullying is always wrong. It's never your fault if you are bullied. If you are being bullied, don't keep it a secret. Tell someone who can help you do something to stop it happening.

I'm Bullied about the Way I Speak

Kurt has moved from one part of the country to another. The children at his new school laugh at the way he speaks. When this happens, he doesn't want to say anything.

Amir's Story

Kurt is the new boy in my class. Everyone laughs at his accent. They don't want to be his friend—just because he's different! I'd like to be his friend, but the other kids might start laughing at me too.

Kurt's Story

I had lots of friends at my old school. Then Dad got a new job and we moved a long way away.

The children at my new school tease me because my accent is different from theirs. Every time I talk they imitate me and laugh!

So now I don't say anything unless I really have to. I don't like being laughed at just because of the way I speak, but they won't stop it.

It's hard to make new friends if you can't say anything!

What Can Kurt Do?

Remember, there's nothing wrong with the way Kurt speaks.
He can:
- ✔ tell his parents,
- ✔ tell his teacher, and
- ✔ not be afraid to speak.

The children will get tired of imitating him every time he talks.

What Kurt Did

I told Mom and she talked to my teacher. He talked to the class about how boring it would be if everyone was exactly like them. He said I make the class much more interesting! We had a class discussion about all the ways people can be different. Now no one imitates me and I talk all the time!

Big Girls at School Hurt Me!

Two older girls want to play with Tamsin every day. They treat her like a little doll. But they frighten Tamsin and sometimes they hurt her.

May's Story

Tamsin never wants to go out to play. She always wants to stay in and clean the classroom. When she does go out, she holds the hand of the grown-up on duty. I wish she'd play with me!

Tamsin's Story

Every day at school, two big girls wait for me on the playground. They chase me and tickle me. They pick me up and swing me around. Sometimes they push and punch me.

They won't stop when I ask them to.

They say it's only a game—but I don't like it. If I cry they call me a crybaby!

If I say I'll tell my teacher, they call me a tattletale!

They won't let me play with my own friends. I feel too frightened to go out to play.

What Can Tamsin Do?

Remember—it's not a game if you aren't having fun.
She can:

✔ tell her friend why she doesn't want to go out to play,

✔ tell her teacher, or

✔ say she wants to play with her own friends and that she wants the big girls to leave her alone.

What Tamsin Did

I told my friend May why I didn't want to go out to play. She said, "You're not a crybaby or a tattletale."

We told my teacher about the big girls and she talked to them. Now the grown-up on playground duty makes sure they leave me alone. I can play with my own friends again.

My Friends Are Bullies

Winnie's friends bully other children and make them unhappy. She knows it's wrong but doesn't try to stop them. Sometimes Winnie joins in. Fern is one of the children they bully.

Fern's Story

I had lice and some girls in my class found out. They told everyone. They said, "Don't go near Fern, you'll get lice!" Everyone kept out of my way. I felt really lonely and miserable.

Winnie's Story

Everyone wants to be in our gang at school because we're really cool! But sometimes my gang bullies other children. I don't like making anyone unhappy. Even though I know it's unkind, I join in because if I didn't, they might bully me! I want to stay part of the gang.

We bullied Fern for having lice. But we've all had lice before. It's not Fern's fault!

I know it's not cool to bully people. I want to stop bullying, but I don't know how.

What Can Winnie Do?

She can:

✔ tell her friends that she doesn't like bullying,

✔ make new friends if the children in the gang still want to be bullies, or

✔ tell her teacher what is happening.

What Winnie Did

I told the gang I wouldn't bully anyone again. They were mad, but Penny agreed with me. Penny and I are best friends now. We aren't part of the gang and we've made new friends like Fern. Together, we stand up for kids who are being bullied. We sometimes even play with the little kids. It isn't cool to bully.

Gus's Story

My friends kept picking on a little kid in the playground. They said they were just teasing him. But when he got upset and cried, they didn't stop. At first I didn't do anything, but I felt bad. Even though I didn't join in, I felt as if I had been bullying him, too.

In the end, I told my friends to leave the little kid alone. I took him to the teacher on duty. My friends stopped picking on him after that.

They Make Fun of My Lunch!

Jade's Story

My mom cooks everything for my lunch box. She won't give me food and drinks in packets and cartons like everyone else has. Every day, some kids grab my lunch box. They open it and say, "What garbage has Jade's mom made for her today?"

They drop my lunch on the floor. Sometimes they throw it away.

I'm always hungry *and* I'm getting skinny!

I hate it when people are rude about my mom. I wish she would give me the same food as everyone else, but she says it's not good for me. I haven't told her what the kids do to my lunch!

What Can Jade Do?

She can:

✔ be proud that her mom is a good cook and that she gives her healthy food,

✔ tell her mom she's being bullied about her lunch, or

✔ tell her teacher what is happening.

What Jade Did

I didn't tell my mom, but I did tell my teacher. She talked to the class about healthy food. We did a class display of healthy foods. We even tried some and everyone liked something. They don't make rude comments about my food or throw it away anymore.

I'm Always in Trouble!

Shelly did well at school. Now she keeps getting into trouble. She gets bad grades for her work. Her parents and friends don't understand what has happened.

Aisha's Story

My friend Shelly writes brilliant stories and can do really hard sums in her head.

She used to get top grades in everything! But suddenly, she's doing really badly. For the first time ever, our teacher said she was disappointed with her work.

I don't know why she's changed.

Shelly's Story

I like doing good work at school. I put my hand up first and I usually know the right answer.

I get lots of stickers and gold stars. But some kids in my class called me "Teacher's pet!" And they started being mean to me.

They hid my books. They threw my school bag in the garbage. They said they'd beat me up if I told anyone. Now I don't work hard or put my hand up anymore.

They laugh at me when I get into trouble—which is all the time!

What Can Shelly Do?

Giving in to the bullies isn't making Shelly happy.

She can:

✔ remember there's nothing wrong with working hard and doing well,

✔ tell her friend Aisha why she is getting bad grades, or

✔ tell her parents and her teacher.

What Shelly Did

I told Mom and Dad about the bullies. They talked to my teacher. They all said I should be proud of doing well.

So I started working hard, but the bullies were worse than before!

So I told my teacher again.

I don't know what she did, but the bullies suddenly stopped bullying me. I'm glad they didn't win.

Homework
Well done

My Friend Bullies His Brother

Nate's story

My friend Marcus bullies his little brother Tommy. Marcus is really popular at school. Everyone wants to be his friend and he's my best friend. He's really nice to me, but he's nasty to Tommy. Sometimes he even hurts him and makes him cry.

He always does it when his mom and dad aren't there. He makes Tommy promise not to tell them.

It's like he can be two different people—good friend Marcus and bully big brother Marcus.

I wish he'd be nice to Tommy.

What Can Nate Do?

He can:

✔ tell Marcus he's being unkind to his brother,

✔ ask Marcus how he thinks Tommy feels, and

✔ be nice to Tommy when he is at Marcus's house and stand up for him.

What Nate Did

I told Marcus I thought he was being awful to Tommy. I tried to make sure Marcus didn't bully Tommy when I was around. Marcus was cross with me. He said Tommy was really annoying and that it was all right for me, I didn't have to live with Tommy.

But now he's started to be kinder so I'm really glad I said something.

Marcus's Story

Tommy, age 8 months

I was the only child for a long time. Then Tommy arrived. Mom and Dad gave him *all* the love and attention. I wished Tommy had never been born and we could go back to the way we were before. I didn't realize I was bullying Tommy until Nate made me think. I don't like bullies!

Anyway, I suppose it's not Tommy's fault. Now that I'm trying to be nicer to Tommy, he isn't quite so annoying!

How to Get Help if You Are Being Bullied

If you are being bullied, you can feel very lonely. If you talk to someone, they can help you. You could talk to your mom or dad or another grown-up in your family, your brother or sister, or a friend.

Your school will have a policy on what to do about bullying, so you could talk to your teacher.

You may think that telling someone will only make things worse. If so, you can:
✔ call the crisis hotline, and
✔ visit Web sites (see page 31).

Remember, bullying is always wrong. You don't have to put up with it.

We Beat Bullying

Ryan used to bully Jacob, even though they were friends. Jacob was afraid of Ryan.

Jacob: When I was new at school, Ryan made friends with me. At first, I was really pleased to have a friend.

Ryan: I didn't have any friends because I was a bully! Jacob didn't know that because he was new.

Jacob: At first, it was great. We did things together at school and went over to each other's houses to play.

Ryan: I started to bully Jacob. I made him do everything I told him. I said I'd beat him up if he told on me or stopped being my friend.

Jacob: Ryan frightened me and he wouldn't let me have any other friends. I wanted to stop being his friend but I didn't know how. In the end, I told my mom and dad.

Ryan: Jacob's mom and dad came to talk to my mom and dad about me bullying Jacob. I was really angry. I thought—I'll get Jacob for this!

Jacob: I was glad I told Mom and Dad, but I was afraid Ryan would get me, just like he said he would if I told anyone.

Ryan: To make things worse, my parents talked to my teacher! She told me that Jacob was only my friend because he was afraid of me. She made me say sorry to Jacob. She said if I "got" him, she'd know about it!

Jacob: After that I just wanted to keep out of Ryan's way. But Ryan really changed and he tried to be nice to me.

Ryan: I didn't want to bully kids into being my friends anymore. I wanted to have real friends who actually liked me. So I had to get nicer!

Jacob: It took a bit of time, but Ryan and I are friends again. We've both got other friends too. The best thing is, Ryan isn't a bully anymore and I'm not being bullied.

Glossary

Bullying
Bullying is when someone hurts you or makes you unhappy and afraid on purpose.

Gang
A gang is a group of friends who hang out together and play together.

Giving in
You give in to someone when they make you do something you don't want to do.

Lonely
You can feel lonely when you don't have many friends and spend a lot of time on your own.

Policy
A policy is a set of ideas and rules. A school bullying policy sets out what should be done if anyone is being bullied at school.

Popular
Someone is popular when people like them and they have a lot of friends.

Proud
You feel proud when you are pleased with something you have done and are happy for other people to know about it.

Secret
When you have a secret, you keep something to yourself and don't tell anyone about it.

Share
You share when you tell or give things to other people and you don't keep things to yourself.

Unkind
You are unkind when you do or say something that makes someone else unhappy.

Further Information

For Kids:
National Youth Crisis Hotline
1-800-448-4663

http://www.kidshealth.org/kid/feeling/emotion/bullies.html
Learn about bullies and how to deal with them.

http://pbskids.org/itsmylife/friends/bullies/
Advice about how to respond to bullies and what actions to take so the bullying stops.

http://www.stopbullyingnow.hrsa.gov/index
Watch web cartoons that help you understand bullying and get tips for preventing bullying.

For Parents:
http://www.kidshealth.org/parent/emotions/behavior/bullies.html
Tips for parents about how to help if their children are being bullied.

http://www.mayoclinic.com/health/bullying/MH00126
Experts at the Mayo Clinic recommend how to help your child handle a bully at school.

http://mentalhealth.samhsa.gov/15plus/parent/
The National Mental Health Information Center offers information for parents and other caregivers to help children deal with bullies.

For Teachers:
http://www.teachablemoment.org/toolbox/toughtimestoolbox.html
This site offers tips for addressing tough issues in your classroom and for helping kids express their feelings.

Note to parents and teachers: Every effort has been made by the publishers to ensure that these Web sites are suitable for children, that they are of the highest educational value, and that they contain no inappropriate or offensive material. However, because of the nature of the Internet, it is impossible to guarantee that the contents of these sites will not be altered. We strongly advise that Internet access is supervised by a responsible adult.

Index

Notes for Parents, Caregivers, and Teachers

When children are bullied, they need adult support to help them deal with it. But they are often reluctant to talk about it. Depression, low self-esteem and poor results at school can be signs that they are being bullied.

• Adults can look out for signs that a child is being bullied.
• Children need to know that being bullied is not their fault.
• Bullying should always be taken seriously.
• Fear of making things worse can stop children from telling anyone. They need to know that it's best to tell an adult, who will take effective action where necessary.

Page 4 Maria's Story
Maria is feeling lonely and left out of her group of friends at school.
• Knowing what makes a friend a good friend can help children to choose their friends well and to be a good friend to other children.

Page 9 Kurt's Story
Kurt is unhappy because the children at his new school laugh at him for being different.
• Understanding that being different is not wrong can help children to appreciate other people and to build their own self-confidence.

Page 12 Tamsin's Story
Tamsin is frightened to go out to play at school because bigger children are bullying her.
• Children need effective intervention from an adult if they are being bullied by bigger children.

Page 15 Winnie's Story
Winnie's friends are bullies. She knows it's wrong to join in but doesn't know how to stop.
• Adults can make it clear that bullying is unacceptable and never cool, and support a child who wants to stop bullying.

Page 19 Jade's Story
Jade is being bullied because she brings healthy food to school for lunch.
• Being different, for example by eating healthy food, is not wrong. An adult can help tackle the bullies and protect the child who is different.

Page 22 Shelly's Story
Shelly is deliberately doing badly at school so that other children don't call her 'teacher's pet'.
• It's hard for children to stand up to bullies on their own. An adult can support children and help them not to give in to bullies.

Page 25 Nate's Story
Marcus doesn't realize he is bullying his little brother.
• Children can be bullies without meaning to be. An adult can point out what they are doing and help them to change their behavior.

Page 28 Ryan and Jacob's Story
Children could role-play the parts in this simple script and then discuss what happened to each character, including possible reasons why Ryan was a bully and what it did to his friendships.